Me and My Dad!

For daddy bears everywhere
A R

For Jeff, for your love and encouragement
A E

ISBN-13: 978-0-545-08185-6
ISBN-10: 0-545-08185-3

Text copyright © 2007 by Alison Ritchie.
Illustrations copyright © 2007 by Alison Edgson.
All rights reserved. Published by Scholastic Inc., 557 Broadway, New York, NY 10012,
by arrangement with Little Tiger Press, an imprint of Magi Publications.
SCHOLASTIC and associated logos are trademarks and/or registered trademarks of Scholastic Inc.

12 11 10 9 8 7 6 5 4 3 2 1   8 9 10 11 12 13/0

Printed in the U.S.A.   40

This edition first printing, January 2008

Me and My Dad!

Alison Ritchie

illustrated by Alison Edgson

SCHOLASTIC INC.
New York Toronto London Auckland Sydney
Mexico City New Delhi Hong Kong Buenos Aires

My dad wakes me up
every morning, like this —
He tickles my nose and
gives me a kiss.

We go out exploring,
there's so much to see.
My dad knows where all
the best secrets will be!

My dad is a giant —
up here so am I !
I stretch really high
until I touch the sky.

We find sticky honey,
our favorite snack.
Watch my dad run when the
bees want it back!

My dad twirls me 'round
and the world whizzes past.
My head gets all dizzy,
I'm spinning so fast!

When loud thunder roars
and the skies turn to gray,
My dad keeps me safe,
till the storm goes away.

Dad does a rainy-day,
staying-dry trick —
To dodge all the raindrops
we have to be quick!

We race to the river
and Dad jumps straight in.
I climb on his back
and we go for a swim.

My dad is so strong,
he can lift anything.
I hope I'm strong, too, when
I'm grown-up like him.

When I get sleepy,
Dad gives me a hug
And carries me home,
all cozy and snug.

We cuddle up close
and as day turns to night,
My dad tells me stories
beneath the starlight.

My dad is the best
daddy bear there could be.
We're together forever —
my dad and me.